2003

For Theresa and Will
—N.C.H.

For Yücel and Emine
—B.E.

Text copyright © 2000 by Nancy Christensen Hall   Illustrations copyright © 2000 by Buket Erdogan

Orchard Books, A Grolier Company, 95 Madison Avenue, New York, NY 10016

Manufactured in the United States of America. Printed and bound by Phoenix Color Corp.
Book design by Eleanor Kwei
The text of this book is set in 30 point Comic Sans.
The illustrations are acrylic on canvas.
1 3 5 7 9 10 8 6 4 2

Library of Congress Cataloging-in-Publication Data
Hall, Nancy Christensen.
Mouse at night / by Nancy Christensen Hall ; pictures by Buket Erdogan.
p.   cm.
Summary: While Miss Bumbly sleeps, Mouse enjoys watching TV, cooking, and generally having
the run of her house—until it is time to make breakfast and return to his mouse hole.
ISBN 0-531-30260-1 (trade only : alk. paper)
[1. Mice Fiction.] I. Erdogan, Buket, ill. II. Title.
PZ7.H1474Mo   2000   [E]—dc21   99-27779

MOUSE AT NIGHT

BY Nancy Christensen Hall
PICTURES BY Buket Erdogan

Orchard Books ● New York

Everything might look quite
normal in Miss Bumbly's house,

but late at night, when the moon is full, things aren't ordinary at all....

"Is it breakfast time already?"